A Twisted Thanksgiving Holiday

DEANN SCLEIL

Cover Designer: Dezignzbybritt

Editor: Moths and Manuscripts Editing

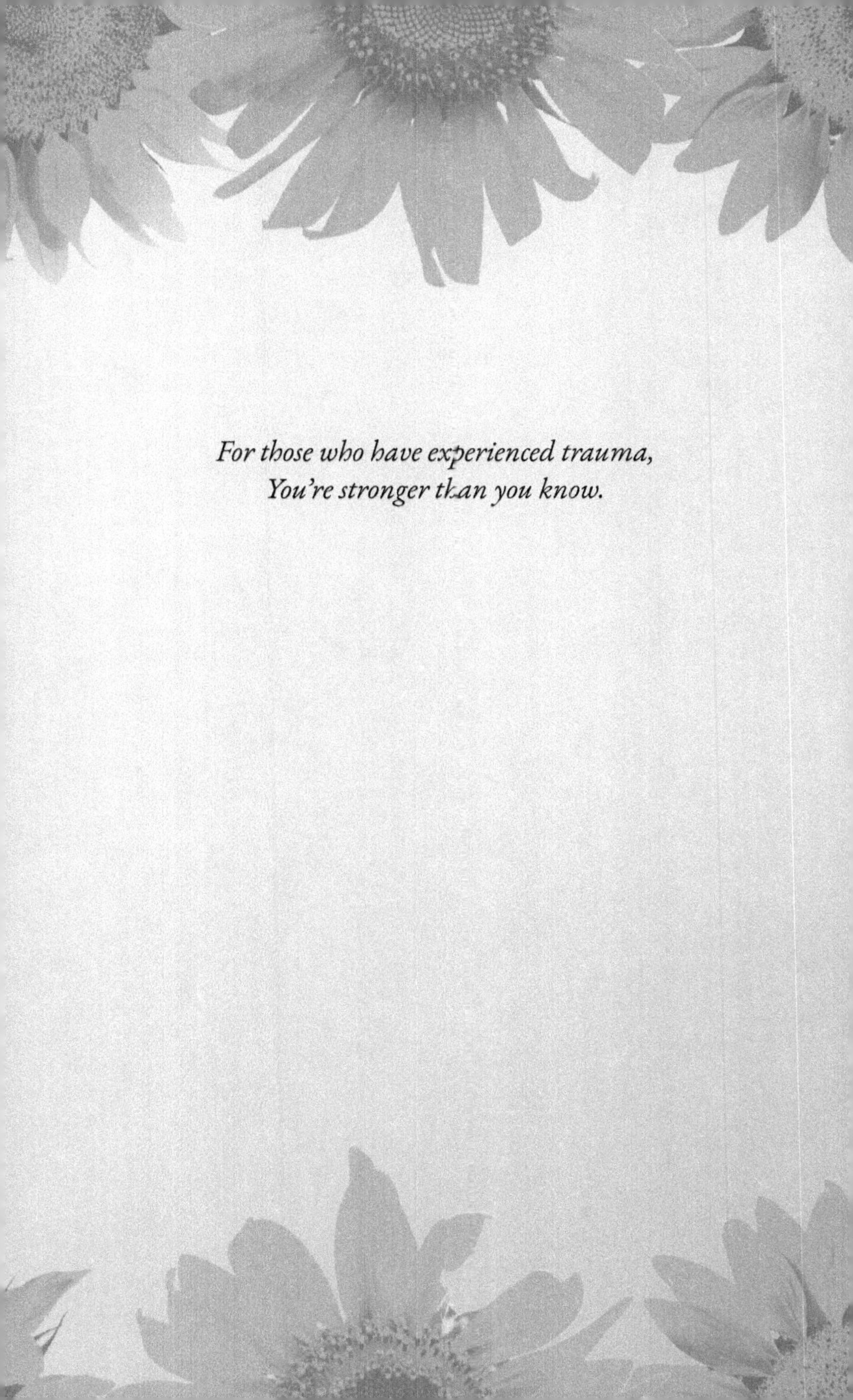

For those who have experienced trauma,
You're stronger than you know.

Contents

Blurb

After years of being mistreated, I finally packed a bag and returned back to my hometown as everyone gathered for the Thanksgiving holiday.

I didn't know what to do, where to go, or who to turn to... until I ran into him.

Joel White. He's twice my age, off-limits, and none other than my father's best friend.

He offers me a place to stay and helps me get back on my feet, but the temptation to get closer to him is hard to avoid.

One night changes everything.

Do I tell him my new secret, or do I go back on the run?

Content Warnings

Age Gap (25/45)
Father's Best Friend
Touch her and die
Forbidden Romance
Secret Relationship
She's off limits
Pregnancy from Violent Relationship
Domestic Violence
Sexual Assault
Mental Health Representation
Mention of suicidal ideation
Mention of self-harm
Brief mention of past miscarriage (Not from FMC)
Soft Cliffhanger

Playlist

Lose Control - Teddy Swims
Rock and a Hard Place - Bailey Zimmerman
For Tonight - Givëon
Are You Even Real - Teddy Swims & Givëon
Escapism - Raye
Survivor - Destiny's Child
Rise Up - Andra Day
Fighter - Christina Aguilera
Latch - Disclosure (Feat. Sam Smith)
ICU - Coco Jones
Safe - Cardi B (Feat. Kehlani)
Dream - Elle Eliades

Prologue: Victoria

Trigger Warnings: Domestic Violence

I have had enough of being treated like trash by the one person who should care about me above anything else.

Being with Chase has had its ups and downs, but mainly downs.

We met each other at sixteen years old and have been together ever since. Out of all these years, I have seen both the good and bad side of him. But I never worked up the courage to leave him.

Most times he uses my body as his personal punching bag when he doesn't get what he wants. Last month it was so bad that I went to the hospital where he made me say I fell down the stairs. I ended up having broken ribs and a concussion. The medical team made every effort to get me alone to ask me what truly happened, but Chase wouldn't let that happen.

The medical team tried to hide the phone number

for the local domestic violence hotline in case I needed it, but somehow, he still ended up finding it when we got home. This just fueled him even more. Once he found it, he beat me so badly that I passed out and didn't wake up until a few days later.

When I woke up, he was right there next to me and said "Baby, I am so sorry. This won't happen again."

I try to believe him when he says that, but it just continues to happen. Those words have lost their meaning to me. I know I should leave and start over, but I won't be able to make it on my own financially.

Chase has broken me so much that I know I should go to therapy. He refuses to let me go anywhere except to and from work. He constantly monitors my location and gets mad if I am not where I am supposed to be. It's worse if I'm late getting home. He makes it difficult for me to live a normal life.

People at work always ask me why I don't go to the police and report the abuse. People don't realize it isn't easy escaping your abuser, especially if he is tracking your every move.

CHAPTER 1

Victoria

**Trigger Warnings: Domestic Violence & Sexual
Assault**

Today has been a long day. Working these shifts at the local diner is exhausting after a while, especially when my body hurts from the physical abuse that I have endured the past few nights.

I already know when I get off work tonight, Chase is going to have a problem. And that side of him, that isn't good, will be brought to the light. My last customer has been taking longer than normal to finish eating and pay, so I am going to be at least ten minutes late to get home.

When my customer is finally finished, I am able to quickly get my side work done and make my way back home. I dread every minute of the drive.

When I pull into the driveway, he is already sitting on the front porch waiting for me with an angry expression on his face. I can see him pacing back and forth with his fists balled up.

This is going to be bad.

"Where have you been?" he yells at me, when I step outside of the car.

Damn, I can't even get two steps before he starts yelling about something that is out of my control. I know trying to explain it won't make a difference to him, but I try anyway.

"I had a customer who took a little longer than normal, so it set me behind on time," I say, knowing he won't care.

He is so angry with me. His face is in a straight line and his cheeks are reddened. "I don't give a fuck about your customer. You know when you're supposed to be home. You should have left when you saw you were going to be late."

"It doesn't work like that-." A harsh slap cuts off the rest of my sentence.

"Don't talk back to me. You need to learn how to keep your mouth shut and do as I say." He grabs me by the arm and pulls me into the house.

I know he's going to leave marks on my skin from how aggressive he is with me.

"I am so tired of you not respecting me and doing the simple things that I ask you to."

This is going to be bad. I can smell the alcohol on him as he continues to yell in my face. Within seconds he pushes me down onto the ground.

"You're." *Kick.* "Going." *Kick.* "To." *Kick.* "Listen." *Kick.* "To" *Kick.* "Me."

The pain that I am feeling is unbearable. I know I am going to have more bruises and broken ribs from his assault. Whenever he drinks alcohol, he doesn't care what he does to me. He uses me like I'm his toy to break.

I need to get out of here before he hurts me more than he already has. I know he'll find me regardless of where I go though.

Once he's done kicking me, I thought that would be the end to his assault, but I realized that was just the beginning. Before I know it, he is forcefully pulling me up and taking me to our bedroom where he forces himself on me.

Each thrust sends more pain through my system. When I go to let out a scream, to tell him to stop, he just covers my mouth and tells me to "take it."

I know I should stop fighting him because he won't stop, no matter how much I beg him to.

I just lay there and let him have his way with me, trying to put my mind into a happy space to distract from the assault on my body.

About ten minutes later, he is finally done.

CHAPTER 2

Victoria

I t's 10:00 PM and I look over to where Chase lays, fast asleep. This is it. My opportunity to try to get out of here and never turn back.

It's important for me to be quiet, and to pack as light as possible. I need to go as far away from here as I can, as quickly as possible.

I slip on some leggings and a hoodie. I grab my wallet and keys, a small bag of clothes, and make my way to the front door. I have been preparing for this moment for as long as I can remember. This is my one chance to be successful at my escape. If not, then I will be trapped here forever, or worse, he will kill me. I creep down the hall to the front door, make my way out, and slowly make my way to my car. I don't even bother shutting the car door all the way because I don't want the noise to wake him.

Quickly I make my way down the street and finally close the car door. I can't believe I have finally left. The other day, I was smart enough to check my car for any trackers to ensure he can't track me outside of the app on my cellphone. He would always remind me that wherever I went, he would find me because of knowing my location.

Luckily, my search came up successful, so he won't be able to find me without a car tracker or me carrying my cellphone with me. I do know he is going to be pissed off when he wakes up and sees that I'm not there anymore, but this is worth it to me.

Chase and I first met in my hometown, which makes it a little risky going back there. With it being a small farm town where everyone knows one another, I should be fine to get immediate help. The drive is about two hours away, but I know I can't go straight to my parents' house because he will look for me there first. Ultimately, I decided to drive straight to the emergency department to be seen.

Two hours go by, and I am approaching the hospital where I see the words emergency department in red. My body is beginning to sweat and I can feel myself being on high alert. I am so afraid to go inside because of this nagging feeling in the back of my mind that Chase will already be here waiting for me, but I know he is probably still fast asleep.

I sit in my car contemplating if I should go in. I feel so vulnerable and have fears that maybe others won't believe what happened. That I won't be able to get the help I need. *Fuck it,* I think to myself. It's almost as if my body is just going through the motions as I make my way out of the car into the hospital.

"Hi, may I get your name, date of birth, and reason

for your visit to get you checked in," the lady at the front desk asks.

I hesitate for a moment wondering if I should be honest or not. Remembering if I lie, someone will know.

"Victoria Maddox. 08.25.1999. Umm...," I begin to say but the nerves start to kick in again.

"Take your time sweetie," the lady says while looking over at me. I know she can probably see some of the bruises on my body.

"I'm sorry, I don't know if I should be here. I'm afraid of what will happen if he finds out that I'm here."

"Here, let me take you back to a room and we can get you settled and make sure you're checked out. I'll also put you under an alias instead of your real name," she says as she points to the direction of where patients go.

As we walk towards the patient area, I notice that she scans her badge to let us in. This makes me feel a little better since the area is at least secured. If he did show up, they wouldn't have my real name. Everywhere I look I feel like there are eyes on me, watching my every move. I might just be overthinking since I'm used to my every move being monitored.

We finally get into my room where the nurse leaves me to sit with my thoughts until she comes back in. *Is this the right thing? Should I tell them everything that happened? Will he kill me if he finds out?*

The thoughts continue to swirl in my head, until the nurse enters the room, pulling me from my thoughts.

"Hi, my name is Caroline, and I will be your nurse today. Is it okay if I take your vitals?" she asks.

I nod my head in approval.

This process goes pretty fast but then we get to the part where I don't know what to say.

"Can you tell me a little about what brought you here today?"

Before words can escape my mouth, tears begin to fall. I knew this would happen sooner or later, but I just can't control it anymore. I feel so much shame that I let this happen to me. I could have gotten out of this so much sooner, but I chose not to. I stayed because I thought things would be different. I believed him when he told me it wouldn't happen again, but I see it was all a lie.

The nurse sits patiently and offers me tissues. "I'm sorry, I just didn't think this day would come where I would be here in this situation. Would it be possible to have a detective come in with the doctor and I can explain everything? I don't think I have it in me mentally to go over this multiple times."

"I understand, I will go make the call and see if we can get someone out here as soon as possible. Is there anything else I can get you in the meantime?"

"May I just get a blanket so I can try to get some rest?"

CHAPTER 3

Victoria

An hour or so goes by when I hear a knock on my door. I awaken to a female detective, the nurse from earlier, and a female doctor.

"Hey sweetie, my name is Detective Anderson. Is it okay if we come in now?"

I feel like I'm at a loss for words, so all I do is nod my head in agreement.

The three of them enter the room with a calming presence. "My name is Doctor Hill, and I will be taking care of you today. Do you mind telling me a little bit about what brought you here, so we can best treat you?"

"I'm not sure where to begin," I hesitated.

"Begin where you most feel comfortable," Detective Anderson says.

With a sigh I let out, "I came home from work a little later than my normal time and my boyfriend lost it. I could barely get into the house before he grabbed me tightly, and pulled me in with him. When we got inside, he got me onto the ground and began to kick me, there wasn't anything that I could do." Tears begin to fall.

"After he finished his physical assault on my body, he brought me to the bedroom where I tried to say no but couldn't fight him off. He raped me and left all of these marks on me. He always would tell me this wouldn't happen again, and that he would change. That never happened. I was always his punching bag, and I could never get any help."

"I want you to know that you are in good hands here and we will do our best to help you get justice. Can you tell me his name and some information about what he looks like and where you live, so I can get that processed in the system?" Detective Anderson asks.

"What if he finds out that I am cooperating with you all, what then?"

"Sweetie, he will not be able to harm you. Once we receive a comprehensive report from the medical team, we can use that to assist you in pressing charges against him. We can also file for a protective order that will prevent him from coming within a certain distance of you."

I let out a sigh. I should trust the detective and medical team because they want to help me. I'm just afraid of the repercussions that can come from moving forward with pressing charges.

After a few minutes of contemplating, I realize I should go ahead and cooperate to help with my safety.

"Chase Holden, 10.22.1999," I say, my voice shaking.

"Thank you, I will look into him while the doctor

proceeds with her exam. I will be back to discuss next steps once I finish looking into everything," Detective Anderson says as she heads to the door.

CHAPTER 4

Victoria

I am so nervous about what is coming next. I love watching all the crime shows on TV, so I have an idea of what will happen. It's just hard for me to believe that I am in this situation where I'm being poked and prodded because of *him*.

"Thank you for being brave today and coming in. I know it can be hard for survivors to seek out help and treatment. But you did. Would you be interested in obtaining a sexual assault forensic exam? This exam will consist of collecting evidence such as your clothing, removing evidence from your mouth and fingernails, swabs, blood tests, and urine tests. All of these items will be documented and run through a lab. During this process we may take photographs of your body to document your injuries as well. This evidence will be available for law enforcement if you wish to make an official police report; however, that will be at your discretion. I can give you a few minutes to think through this process and determine if you would be interested in undergoing this exam," Doctor Hill explains.

I contemplate for a second if I should do it, but before I know it, I am blurting out "let's do it. It's time that I receive justice for the pain that I have been experiencing for so many years."

"Okay. Let me get all that we will need. Caroline will be with us in the room if you need a support person to help you get through this process."

A few minutes pass and Doctor Hill and Caroline are both back in the room with everything to perform the exam.

"If at anytime this becomes too much, then please let us know and we can stop or give you a break. I will explain what we are doing every step of the way, so you are aware of what is going on. I want you to feel as comfortable as possible throughout this process," Doctor Hill says.

I feel a little nervous by all of the swabs and the camera that is in the room. I wish I had someone here with me that I know to help provide me with some comfort during this time, but I know I am strong enough to go through this alone. I have been navigating the stressors of my relationship with Chase for so long, that I can face this exam head on even if it does make me a little nervous.

CHAPTER 5

Victoria

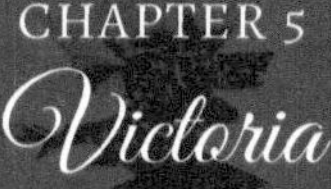

A few hours went by, and we were finally finished with the exam. They gave me a sweatshirt and sweatpants since they took my clothes for the evidence collection process.

There were moments when things became a bit too much and I had to take breaks. Doctor Hill and Caroline were both supportive throughout the whole process. They supported me when I had to take the breaks, and when I began crying. The realization finally hit me. What Chase was doing to me was not right. It wasn't the way I should be treated.

As I start to get settled back in the bed, the detective comes back into the room to give me an update.

"Hey Victoria. I wanted to let you know that I was able to pull up Chase's background and was able to find some past accusations of domestic violence on his record; however, the charges never stuck due to lack of evidence," Detective Anderson said.

Fuck. He has done this before. I don't understand

how I couldn't know. I have been with him for so long that I would have thought that something like this would have come up, but I guess not.

"Can you tell me when this happened? We've been together for ten years now, and I wasn't aware that he was accused of domestic violence."

"I can't tell you the specifics, but what I *can* tell you is these concerns did arise during the timeframe that you two have been together."

I can feel my heart start to beat faster. I can't believe he was doing this to someone else while we were together. This wasn't good, and I feel so bad for the other women. I know all too well what it was like.

"It just doesn't make sense to me. He kept a close eye on me, and he was always home when I got home from work. I don't know how he had the time to do this to someone else. I truly hope that you all will be able to do something about it and help the ones who were involved get justice, the same way that you all are helping me."

"We'll be doing everything we can to help support you and help the others involved. Keep in mind, the justice system does take time. However, based on your injuries and the evidence collected today it can help with the case against him," she says.

Before I can respond, there's a knock on the door followed by Doctor Hill and Caroline entering the room.

"We received the results of your urine test. Is this a good time to share those results?" Doctor Hill asks.

"I can step out while you all go over the results," Detective Anderson begins to say before I interrupt her.

"Please stay. I would like to have another person here with me when I receive the results."

She nods her head in agreement to stay.

"When running your urinalysis there weren't any concerning details that came up. Your PH levels are where they should be; however, there was one result that popped up that is important to go over."

"You're scaring me. Can you just say what the results are? I don't want to be more stressed out surrounding this than I need to be."

"Yes, I'm sorry. Your urine screen shows that you are pregnant. I would like to conduct an ultrasound to see how far along you are, if you are okay with that."

"WHAT THE FUCK. You have got to be kidding me. I was taking my birth control. I know there were a couple days that I missed it, but I didn't think this would happen," I say as tears begin to fall from my eyes.

I am at a total loss for words. This can't be happening right now. I don't want to have to go back to Chase and tell him about his baby. I don't even know if he will be happy about the news, or if he will just take out more anger on me. *Fuck, I don't know what to do.*

"I know this is a lot to process right now. I can come back later and do the ultrasound to give you some time to think about everything," she says.

"No, can we do it now. I want to know how far along I am and if the baby is still alive. I took a bad beating earlier, so I am afraid that the results of the ultrasound might not be a good one."

"Of course. Caroline, can you please grab the ultrasound kit."

A few moments go by before Caroline makes her way back in with the ultrasound cart.

"If you could lay back on the table, I will put the gel on your stomach. It might be a little cold," Doctor Hill says.

I look away as she places the ultrasound belly wand on my stomach. I look away because I'm afraid of seeing what will appear. Before I know it, I hear boom boom boom.

"It appears the baby has a strong heartbeat. This is good news," she says.

She continues to move the ultrasound belly wand around, so I decide to take a look at the screen to see what she's doing. I see a small figure appear on the screen.

"Based on what I am seeing, it appears that you are about twelve weeks pregnant," she says as she begins to wipe off the gel from my stomach.

This is a lot to take in. This is my miracle baby after everything that I have gone through.

"There are different options that are available for you now that we have an idea of how far along you are. I can provide some resources to help with the decision-making process. Take your time though, and don't rush. We will be here to support you, no matter what decision you make," Doctor Hill says.

"Is it possible for me to take a little walk down the

hallway? I need to clear my head and make this decision for myself."

"I am okay with that," Doctor Hill says.

"I'm okay with that too. I will be here when you return," Detective Anderson replies.

CHAPTER 6

Victoria

There is so much to take in. I've barely gotten any sleep, so I'm exhausted. I hope they will allow me to stay a little longer at the hospital since I have nowhere to go. I need to make a plan and determine what next steps to take.

As I leave my room and make my way down the hallway, I hear a familiar voice call my name.

"Is that you Victoria," a male voice calls out.

I turn my head, and I am in sudden disbelief when I see my father's best friend. *Joel White.* I had no idea that he was working in the hospital. I don't want him to see me this way and it gets back to my parents about the condition that I am currently in.

"Hi Joel. Long time, no see," I say as I try to cover myself up, so he doesn't see the bruises.

"How has everything been? I remember when your dad said you were moving away with that boyfriend of yours," Joel says.

"Well, things haven't been the best, but I'm managing."

"Do your folks know that you are back in town?"

"No, I just got back a few hours ago and came right here. Honestly, I don't think I want them to know that I'm back just yet. I am trying to navigate some changes and figure out what next steps there are for me before letting anyone know about my return."

"I get that. Are you okay? It's not often that people pop up in the middle of the night, unless something serious is going on," he says.

I don't know why that triggered something in me, but tears immediately streamed down my face.

He pulls me in for a hug, which makes me flinch at first. "Do you want to go back into your room to talk? If not, I completely understand."

I nod my head in agreement, and we make our way back to my room where Detective Anderson is still present.

CHAPTER 7

Seeing Victoria in the condition that she is in today, breaks my heart. I saw her trying to cover up the bruises and scars that she has. I hope that man didn't do this to her because if I find out he did, I don't know if I could refrain from doing something to him that I shouldn't.

When I was looking at the emergency department room tracker, I didn't see her name appear but now it makes sense. There was a patient listed under no information, so that must have been her.

I can tell I struck a nerve with her when I asked about how she was doing from the way that she broke down in front of me. I feel so bad for her. I want to be able to support her as she navigates whatever is going on. I hope she feels comfortable being able to open up to me.

As we get back into her room, I notice that there's a detective in the room. I don't know what I am getting myself into, but I really hope that she isn't in too much trouble.

"Is everything okay?" Detective Anderson asks when we walk into the room.

"I'm fine. When I was going for my walk, I ran into Joel. He's someone that I grew up around. He had asked if I filled my parents in on what is going on, and I just lost it from there," Victoria says.

I can tell she still feels nervous about me being present. If she went through what I think she did, then she is going to need support. Whether that be from me, or from her family.

"Hi, I'm Joel White. I'm one of the emergency department doctors, but I'm also her father's best friend," I say as I shake the detective's hand.

I don't know if it is right for me to be in the room with Victoria right now since it appears that there is an investigation going on, but if she wants my help then I will be sure to give it to her.

"Is it okay if we talk with Joel in the room," she asks Victoria.

"That's fine. I haven't been able to fill him in on what is going on right now, but I trust him."

It makes me happy knowing that she trusts me with everything going on, even if I haven't seen her in a few years.

Before the detective can start speaking, Doctor Hill enters the room.

"What are you doing here?" she asked me.

"I'm a friend of the family. When I saw her in the hallway, she asked for my support. Don't mind me, I won't be in the way," I say.

"Alright. Victoria would you like Doctor White to

remain in the room as we discuss next steps, or would you like him to step out?"

"Would it be alright if Joel stays? He can provide some comfort that I might not be able to receive elsewhere."

"If you're okay with it, then so am I," she says, directed at me.

I nod in agreement.

CHAPTER 8

"I know you took some time to go for a walk to think about the baby. Have you decided on what route you would like to take? It's completely fine if you still need some more time. We can have a social worker come in, if you would like," Doctor Hill says.

"No thank you. I don't want to confide in another person. I trust you all and would like to continue to work with y'all if that's okay. I decided that I would like to keep the baby. I have no idea what I am doing and how I am going to raise them, but I will figure it out."

"That is great news to hear. We can provide you with some resources for parenting and get you started on a prenatal vitamin to ensure you are getting the proper supplements in your system to carry out a healthy pregnancy. Since we have completed your sexual assault forensic exam, we want to ensure that you have all the resources needed for when we discharge you from the hospital in a little bit."

Fuck. I didn't think about where I would be going after I left the hospital.

"Do you have any domestic violence shelters that have availability? If not, I can look into a hotel."

"She can stay with me," Joel interjects, causing us all to turn our heads to him.

"You know she will need a lot of support throughout the next few months and potentially into the future. She may be triggered by being around a male after she suffered so much pain at the hands of one. Will you be able to ensure that she gets all of the help and support that she needs?" Detective Anderson says.

"Yes, I have an extra bedroom in my house, and it is gated off, so we won't have to worry about anyone getting in to harm her," he says.

"Joel, you don't have to do this. I don't want to be a burden to you and your family," I begin to say before I am cut off.

"You are not a burden. I truly don't mind. I get off my shift in an hour, then I can take you home."

Am I really doing this? Am I really going to intrude in this man's life? He shouldn't feel responsible for me.

"Well, I guess I have a plan then. What do I need to do to get the protective order in place?"

"We went ahead and filed it on your behalf. He should be served soon. In the meantime, please get some rest. We will coordinate with you in time to come to the police station and complete a formal statement, then we can work on pressing charges against him. This will be a long road, but ensuring you have support during it, is what is going to matter the most," Detective Anderson says.

"Thank you all for all of your help today and ensuring that I get all the support and resources that I need."

"Of course. In your discharge summary, I will put more information about what we did today, some OBGYNs to choose from, domestic violence hotline resources, and parenting resources. Please take your time reviewing them, and if you have any questions about any of the information, I am giving you my desk line that you can contact. I will send Caroline in with the discharge paperwork as soon as I am finished."

Detective Anderson leaves her card with me, and the two of them head out of the room for the night.

CHAPTER 9

I didn't realize the severity of everything that Victoria is going through, until this moment where everyone came together to discuss options. I know she said that I don't need to help her, or be there for her, but I want to be. I want to ensure that she's okay and has all the help that she needs. Even if she doesn't want her family to know.

"I am going to be here through everything. If you need a shoulder to cry on, I will be here. If you need someone to yell at, I will be here. If you just need someone to talk to, I will be here. I know this will be an adjustment moving to a new home with everything that you went through, but I will ensure that I make the adjustment as easy as I can."

I can see the tears begin to well up in her eyes. I didn't mean to make her cry, but I want her to know that I will be supportive and be with her every step of the way.

"Thank you, Joel. You have no idea how much this means to me. I really had no idea where I was going to go once I got discharged today. I am thankful that you were able to come into my life. I have been dreading this Thanksgiving season because I was either going to be stuck with my abuser or stuck by myself. Two options that really didn't sound good."

This breaks my heart because I don't want to make her think about the negatives surrounding the holiday. Hopefully, this transition will be good for her and will allow her to start over.

"Maybe we can make new traditions this year. If you want to see your parents and let them know what's going on, then we can navigate that. If you want to just stay in and spend time together, then we can do that too. We have two weeks to figure that out, so don't stress it. Let me go finalize all of my notes, then I will come back in to grab you to head out."

"Thank you. I am going to try to get a little rest if I can while I wait for you."

I head back to my desk and check in with Doctor Hill to ensure that Victoria will be ready to go soon. She thanks me for everything I'm doing for her and reminds me that she is going to need a lot of support with everything that's happened.

After touching base with her, I head back to my desk and finalize everything so I can head out for the night.

Before I know it, Caroline is coming into the room with my discharge paperwork. So much for me being able to get some rest.

"What time is it by chance?"

She looks down at her watch and says "it's 4:45. I'm sorry we have kept you so long. I hope you were able to get some sleep in between us coming in and out of your room."

Dang, I have been here so long. I feel so tired and can't wait until I get to climb into a nice warm bed and not have to worry about anything happening to me. I know I have a safe space with Joel, even if I haven't seen him in a few years.

It's just crazy how supportive he wants to be of me. I didn't see a wedding ring on his finger, so I hope whoever he is living with won't feel any type of way about me crashing in their home.

I start to remove those thoughts from my mind as Caroline begins to go through the discharge summary.

My instructions seem simple enough to properly take care of myself and my little human that I'm growing inside of me.

"Hey Vic, you ready to go," Joel says as he makes his way through the door.

"I'm as ready as I can be. I'm just ready to crash, it's been a long night."

"You can sleep on the way back to my house. It is about a thirty-minute drive from the hospital," he says.

Part of me is nervous about what is to come and how this interaction with him is going to be. On the other hand things have never been awkward between the two of us, so it should be fine.

We make our way to his car in the staff parking lot, and I'm on high alert that Chase knows where I am. He has to have realized that I left already. After speaking with Joel in the hospital, I found out that my parents have moved, but I'm not sure where they live yet. This means Chase won't either because we were under the impression they were at the same house as before. He also shouldn't know where Joel lives, I just need to keep reminding myself of that.

After looking around the lot, Joel grabs my hand. "It's okay Vic, I got you and he can't hurt you."

I nod and keep my head down as we quickly approach his vehicle. I should have known that he would be driving a pickup truck. He's always been the type of guy that gives off country vibes. He is also a gentleman since he opens the passenger side door for me to climb in.

"Thank you. If you don't mind, I'm going to close my eyes and hopefully get a little bit of sleep."

"Go ahead, you deserve it after everything you have been through today. I'll wake you up once we arrive at my house," he says.

With that, I close my eyes and doze off into a slumber.

CHAPTER 11

Chase

I move my arm on Victoria's side of the bed and realize she is not there. I can see her cellphone, so I know she has to be somewhere in this house. I slide out of bed and notice that she is not in the bathroom or the kitchen, which is weird for her. I decide to pop my head outside and notice that her vehicle is missing.

This fucking bitch.

She knows better than to up and leave the house without asking for permission and letting me know where she's going. I don't know why she thinks that she can just go wherever she wants to, whenever she wants to.

Over the past few weeks, I had been contemplating putting a tracking device on her car, but I knew she wouldn't do anything to betray me. Obviously, I thought wrong. At this point, she could be anywhere. Maybe she was stupid enough to go back to her parents' house. If she did, then that's going to be my first stop.

Since it is only a two-hour drive and it's 5:00 in the

morning, I can head that way and be there as the sun begins to rise. When I locate her, she is going to wish that she never left this house without me. She thinks what I did to her last night was bad, just wait until she sees what I am going to do to her now.

 Victoria

"Vic, wake up. We're home," Joel says as he slightly taps me on my shoulder.

Home. This is not my home; this is his home. I am just a visitor.

I open my eyes and see the huge house come into view in front of me. I know they say doctors make good money, but I didn't think enough to live in such a lavish home. I'm too tired to ask questions. I'll figure that out after I get a good night's rest.

Before I know it, he is coming over to my side of the truck and opens the door for me to step out.

"Let's head inside. I can show you where your room is, I'll also get you a t-shirt and towel so you can shower when you are ready."

"Yes please. I need one after what I went through at home and in the hospital."

He nods and escorts me to the front door.

When we make our way inside, it is so quiet in here

that I don't want to make a peep to wake up the others in here.

"Can I have a glass of water please," I say in a whisper when we get into the foyer.

"You can, but why are you whispering? You can talk in a normal tone."

"I don't want to wake anyone up here. It is bright and early in the morning."

He begins to let out a laugh, but I really don't know what's funny.

"There's nobody else here outside of you and I, so you can talk as loud as you want to," he says.

I feel so dumb now, because I thought I would be impeding on his life and whoever he lives with. When in reality there was nobody ever here. I don't know why I always assume things instead of just asking questions straight outright. Maybe it's because Chase never let me ask questions. It was always do as he says and don't ask any questions pertaining to it.

"Hey, are you good over there? You seemed to tune out briefly."

Shoot, he noticed.

"Yeah, I'm good. I just expected someone like you would be settled down at this point. You seem like a successful doctor and what I've seen so far of your home, it is amazing."

"I wish I was with someone. It's been a journey, but I put a lot of my focus on work and the farm so I haven't found someone that can put up with my schedule."

"Did you just say farm? As in one with animals?" I question with my mouth hanging open.

"Yes animals, that's what a farm is," he says with a laugh.

I punch him in the arm "hey, be nice. I will have to look around more when I wake up." I let out a laugh.

"I did decide to take off the rest of the work week to be here for you and help you get things in place. We can definitely take a little tour around the farm later today. For now, let's go get you settled."

We make our way up to the second floor of the house and he shows me where my bedroom is. It feels good to know I have my own space.

"Here is where you will be sleeping. If you need me, my bedroom is on the opposite side of the hall," he says as he points into the direction of his bedroom.

"Wow, thank you. Where is the bathroom so I can go get showered?"

We walk down the hallway to the bathroom. He grabs a towel for me and an oversized t-shirt and boxers that I can wear to bed.

"After we wake up, we can get you some clothes, so you can be comfortable. If you need anything in the meantime, I will be in my bedroom taking a shower as well."

"Thank you," I say as I make my way into the bathroom, closing the door behind me.

I turn the water up until it reaches the perfect temperature. I slide off the clothes that the hospital gave me and make my way into the shower. It's the perfect size where I can spread out and not have to worry about being cramped, like I was in our shower back home.

As the water washes over my skin, I examine my body

and see the purple and blue bruises everywhere. I have been living this way for so long and can't believe what I am seeing on myself. I also don't know how I didn't realize that I was pregnant. I know I have had sensitive nipples and some nausea, but I never would have imagined that I was pregnant.

All of the feelings and thoughts begin to overwhelm me and the tears start pouring down my face. I keep trying to mentally tell myself that I am not a victim. I am a survivor. I survived my abuser. I know it is going to be a long road to recovery, but I know I can do it. Later in the day, I will start my healing journey and find resources that can help me navigate the challenges that I have experienced over the past ten years.

I am so scared of what is to come. I try to pull myself together so I can finish getting showered and rinse off what he did to me. Once I finish, I throw on the shirt and boxers that Joel gave me. They are definitely too big, but they will do the job while I sleep.

As I make my way to my bedroom, I see Joel's bedroom light is on. I hesitate for a moment and don't know if I should go to my own room or go into his.

CHAPTER 13

Joel

Bringing her back to my home today has been doing something to me. It is so weird to think she's the daughter of my best friend. I know I have to respect her boundaries and not tell him that she is with me, but it's easier said than done.

Sitting in the hospital room with her when the medical team and detective were talking about next steps, made me realize how bad things have been going for her. I don't think people around her even knew what was happening, because it was rare that she would come home.

I hope now that she is back home, she will be willing to connect with her family again. I know I need to keep her safe for now, because I don't want anything to happen to her.

After I hop out my shower, I make my way over to my bed where I scroll through the news from today. There doesn't seem to be anything interesting going on in our community, so I decide it's time to get some rest before we have to tackle all the tasks that need to be done.

Right as I go to turn the light off, I hear a knock on my door.

"Joel, can I come in?" A low voice says.

I hop out of bed and make my way over to the door. "Are you okay?"

I can see her red eyes, as if she was recently crying. It's almost as if she knows that I can see her feelings because the tears begin to stream down her face again.

"Come on, let's go sit on the bed," I say. I gently grab her hand and move her in that direction. She looks so beautiful in my t-shirt, but I need to focus on her and how she's feeling right now.

When we get onto the bed, she instantly leans into me, gasping in between words. "I'm so sorry. I thought I was stronger than this, but I don't want to be alone tonight. Can I please lay in here tonight? I won't take up space."

"Of course you can," I say, pulling the sheets back for her to get under. "I will be right here, if you need anything."

She ends up laying against my chest and cries herself to sleep. I feel so useless in this moment. I don't know how to give her the comfort she needs.

I turn off the light and before I know it, I drift off to sleep as well.

CHAPTER 14

Victoria

Trigger Warnings: Mention of Suicide and Self-Harm

I wake up in the middle of the day screaming with a nightmare of Chase kicking me, causing me to lose the baby.

Joel jolts up out of bed. "Is everything okay Vic?" He says half awake.

"I'm sorry. I had a nightmare that I was back in that house with Chase and he was doing terrible things to me."

"You're safe here. I won't let him hurt you. If he comes near you, then it will be the last decision he makes for himself."

He looks over at the clock, "It's ten in the morning, come here and try to get some more sleep."

I do as he says and lean into him as he rubs my arm up and down to calm me from my nightmare.

I've been keeping the extent of my injuries and how

long I have been undergoing abuse from him, I just don't know how he will react when he finds out. Maybe I should just go back on the run again, but for some odd reason I do trust that I will be safe with him.

Being cuddled up in Joel's arms and feeling his touch makes me want to give in to him, even though that's not his intention right now. His number one priority is making sure that I am in a safe environment where Chase can't get me. But the what ifs of what he will think if he sees the marks and bruises under my shirt constantly runs through my thoughts.

I'm not the beautiful woman most guys go after. In fact, I'm the opposite. I'm the ugly, broken woman that guys try to stay far away from. When I was surrounded by Chase everyone saw how possessive he was of me, which made me feel like I truly was wanted by someone. His actions, on the other hand, showed that I should want anyone but him.

I just need to clear my head and try to go to sleep since these constant thoughts running through my mind aren't going to help me. It's only going to make things worse and drag me deeper into the depression I've fallen in.

One thing about Chase was he wouldn't let me obtain mental health treatment when I knew I needed it. There were moments that I felt suicidal. I didn't know what to do. I tried to overdose on Ibuprofen, but realized that it just messed with my body and didn't lead me to ending my life. There were days that I would turn to cutting as a way to release my emotions, but nothing ever seemed to work.

As I lay here reflecting on my past and everything that's happened, I know when I wake up I need to figure out what counseling resources are available to me. It's almost as if Joel knows that I'm overthinking things right now because he leans over and plants a kiss on my forehead and says "baby girl, it's going to be okay. Close your eyes and try to get some rest. We can work through things once we wake back up."

"Thank you," is all I can mutter before I close my eyes and drift back to sleep.

CHAPTER 15

Chase

I don't know if I am more irritated that Victoria left or the fact that I can't find her.

When I got to her hometown, I went to the house where her parents supposedly lived, but it turns out they don't live there anymore. That pissed me off more since I thought it would be easy to locate her.

After all these years, she has never been brave enough to just walk away from me. I don't understand why she thought she could do it this time. I really don't know where to go from here. There aren't too many places that I remember her frequenting, which makes this so much harder to navigate.

All I know is that when I get my hands on her, it will be the last time she runs away from me.

CHAPTER 16

Victoria

After a few more hours of sleep, I finally wake up and realize that I am still in Joel's bed, but he isn't here. I take a moment to gain my composure since I remember everything that was running through my head at the hospital. I know I can't lay in bed all day, so I pull myself together and make my way downstairs.

As I head down the steps, the smell of eggs and bacon fill my nose. I don't know when the last time I had breakfast cooked for me.

"Good afternoon Vic. How'd you sleep?" Joel says as I round the corner into the kitchen.

"I slept well. Thank you for letting me share your bed with you. I don't think I can be alone right now as I navigate everything that's happened within the past 24 hours."

"I know we haven't talked about what all happened, but if at any time you want to talk about it we can," he says, sliding over a cup of orange juice and a plate of food to me.

"Thank you. I do think I want to get started with therapy. I've been wanting to do it for a long time now, but Chase never allowed me to. He would always say that I didn't need it, so I started to believe what he was saying. Would you be able to help connect me with a virtual therapist? I don't think I am ready to just be out and about because he might come looking for me."

"Of course. Today I can go out and pick up a laptop, new phone, and clothing for you. Just make me a list of your sizes and anything else that you need."

AFTER WE FINISH EATING I GO AHEAD AND MAKE my list of things that I need Joel to get:

- ◯ Medium T-Shirts
- ◯ Medium Pants (Leggings Preferred)
- ◯ Medium Hoodies
- ◯ Medium Long Dress
- ◯ Medium Pajama Sets (Long & Short Sleeves)
- ◯ Medium Panties (briefs) & sports bras
- ◯ A few maternity outfits
- ◯ Shoes: Size 9 (Black boots, sneakers, & slippers)
- ◯ Socks: Size 9
- ◯ Toiletries
- ◯ Journal and Pen
- ◯ Laptop and E-Reader
- ◯ Fuzzy Blanket

I feel bad asking for so much, but I need to get my life back in order since I'm starting all over again.

"Here's my list. I will find a way to pay you back for everything once I get back on my feet," I say as I hand over the list to Joel.

"Vic, please do not worry about trying to pay me back. I wanted you to come stay with me. You don't owe me anything. I'm here to help you get back on your feet and ensure that you have what you need."

This is going to be hard for me since I always feel like I owe money to Chase if he decides to buy me anything that I want, even though I am the one working for the items. I guess I need to stop comparing Joel to Chase since they don't appear to be anything alike.

"Okay, if you say so. Do you mind if I watch some TV until you get back? Maybe after that you can give me a tour around the farm."

"You don't have to ask me if you can watch TV. You live here now, feel free to do whatever you would like. Also, yeah when I get back we can walk around and get you familiar with everything. I should be back in two hours with everything."

I head to the living room and plop down on the couch and turn on some reality TV. This should hopefully help pass the time while I wait for him to return.

CHAPTER 17

When I woke up today Victoria was fast asleep next to me in bed. It took her a little to calm down, but I'm glad she was able to feel safe. Part of me knows that being cuddled up with her each night is dangerous. There's something about her that is just pulling me to her. The goal of her being in my home is to make sure that she's safe, not to develop feelings for her. However, I'm not sure if I can hold back if we get close.

I decided to make her some breakfast today because she has been through a lot. As she moved around to get comfortable in bed, I noticed some of the bruises that coated her skin even though she tried to hide them. The anger that built inside me at seeing them makes me want to hurt whoever did this to her, in the same way they did to her.

I would buy this girl the world if it ensures that she will be okay. I *want* to be able to treat her to things that she might not have been exposed to in the past. When I asked her to make a list of items that she wanted me to pick up from the store, I was expecting her to put down so much more. But she didn't.

I've never had to shop for a lady before, so this is going to be an interesting time at the store. I'm also going to spoil her and grab other things that I hope she likes. I want her to have things that will bring her joy and happiness, so if that is grabbing items that she can use for comfort then I will.

As I am perusing the stores I have no idea what her style is, so I pick out a little bit of everything. I choose some t-shirts, sweaters, leggings, jeans, sweater dresses, and undergarments in different colors and designs that hopefully she'll like. Shopping for undergarments was a pain in the ass. There's so many different types of panties, how is a guy supposed to know which ones to get. She said briefs, but I'm not sure if women like a specific color or kind of briefs.

I run into a lady who appears to be the same age as Vic to get some advice.

"Excuse me, can I get some help please?" I ask the lady.

Confusion appears across her face when she says "I don't work here so I don't think I can be of much help."

"I know, I was just wondering if you could help me figure out what undergarments to get for someone around your age. She doesn't have anything and I want to get her some items to get her back on her feet."

"Oh yeah, let me show you what options would be best."

We make our way to the undergarment area and she helps me pick out some briefs and sports bras. I thank her for all of her help and head to the electronics section where I'm more comfortable. I grab her a laptop, e-reader, and phone from this section, then make my way over to the stationary area where I pick out a journal and some different pens she can use.

With her being pregnant I decide to pick up some neutral onesies and a pregnancy journal that she can use to track how things are going. I also came across a necklace that says *mama* on it, so I grab that for her too.

After I getting the rest of the items on her list, I finally checkout and make my way back home.

CHAPTER 18

As I sit on the couch waiting for Joel to return, I think about how I'm going to be a mom to this baby. I feel like I'm too broken to be a single mother, but if I have Joel's support it may help me a little. I just want the best life for my baby.

My mind keeps bouncing back and forth on if I should try to raise the baby, or if I should put them up for adoption. I think as my pregnancy progresses I will be able to finally make the decision on what I will do. Maybe I should sit down with Joel and tell him everything that has happened because it doesn't feel right to keep this a secret from him when I'm under his roof.

I'm drawn out of my thoughts when the sound of the door closing startles me. When I see it's just Joel I calm down a little, but I know I'm going to remain on edge until Chase is caught.

"Did you buy the whole store?" I say with a laugh when I see all of the bags in his hands.

"Maybe a little. I still have bags in the car."

This man really is going to spoil me when he doesn't have to.

"I wanted to make sure you have everything that you need and some more. I bought you some chocolate to help with pregnancy cravings too," he says.

He is such a sweetheart.

"I will do anything you need me to. I'm going to grab the rest of the bags. Find something to wear, then we can head out to the stables when I return."

As he makes his way to the car, I look through all the different clothes that he bought me. Shockingly, he has some good taste and bought me exactly what I would have picked out myself. I grab a pair of leggings, a hoodie, underwear, socks, and some boots to make sure that I stay warm with the weather continuously dropping. I make my way to the bathroom and change quickly since I can't wait to see what else this spacious home entails.

A FEW MINUTES LATER, I MAKE MY WAY BACK out to the living room. Joel is standing there in his jeans, hoodie, and cowboy boots. *This man is to die for.*

"Are you ready to head outside?" He asks, pulling me out of my thoughts of him.

"Yeah, you lead the way."

We make our way to the backdoor that leads us out

to the field behind the house. I am amazed by all of the land that he has. I can see stables and some of the horses roaming the field, that I can't wait to get to know.

I follow closely behind him as we enter the stables. There is one horse that stands out to me the most. It has a brown coat and is just so pretty. I can tell Joel sees the horse that I'm eyeing when he says, "That's Cash. He is one of the newer horses on my property. I recently rescued him from an owner who no longer wanted him. It was a sad story, but I'm glad he is now at a home where he will be taken care of."

"Can I pet him?" I don't even know if that is the proper terminology when it comes to horses, but it sounds right.

"Is it okay if I guide your hand?" He asks.

I nod in agreement. Joel grabs my right hand and guides it to the top of Cash's head. He slowly moves my hand along the front of his head to get me acclimated with the horse.

"Sometimes Cash has a hard time adjusting to others' touches; however, he seems to be fine with yours."

Maybe I found a new companion that I will be able to spend time with when I need it.

"Will it be okay if I spend a few minutes with him, then I'll catch up with you after?" I ask.

"Yeah, I will be right over here getting the other horses fed. You can brush him if you would like to." He says, handing over a brush.

When Joel goes over to the other horses, I slowly brush along the side of Cash. I decided to take a few minutes to express my feelings and get things off my chest.

"Hey buddy. It sounds like you and I both came from some unpleasant situations. I want you to know that I will be here to help support you as long as Joel allows me to. I might not be able to ride you with me being pregnant right now, but I will make sure I come out here every day to just spend time with you. I'm afraid that the man who harmed me will find me again. He hurt me so bad, and I just don't know how I'm going to move forward from this. Joel seems like a great man, but I know I'm off-limits to him with him being my father's best friend. That's another challenge. How am I supposed to tell my parents about all the bad things that Chase did to me? How am I supposed to move on and raise the baby of my abuser? I just don't know what to do or how I'm going to move on from here. I guess I need to be strong for myself and my baby." I tell him as tears start to fall from my cheeks.

As I was talking, I noticed Joel kept stealing small glances in my direction. Now that the waterworks have begun and I can't hide them, he quickly comes over to me.

"Hey Vic. Are you okay?" He asks, pulling me into a hug.

"No, I'm not. I think it's time that we sit down, and I tell you everything that is going on. I've tried to keep the extent of what happened a secret because I don't want you to look at me differently. I can't do it anymore, unless I go back on the run."

"You're not going anywhere. What happened to you is not going to change anything. You are safe here and I will continue to provide everything that you need. Let's head inside and have this talk."

I nod in agreement as tears keep running down my face.

CHAPTER 19

LATER THAT DAY

Victoria and I spent about two hours talking through everything that happened with Chase. She told me the events leading up to her going to the hospital and what has been going on over the past ten years since she has been in a relationship with him.

If I get my hands on him, he will wish that he never came after her. She is the sweetest person that I know, and she doesn't deserve to go through what she did with him.

We talked about her pregnancy and the options that she was thinking about, but she ultimately decided that she wanted to keep the baby. I agreed to help her raise the baby, so she doesn't have to do it alone. She agreed. I don't know what this means for us, but I hope it allows her to realize that I am not going to let her fail or get hurt again.

After the conversation, I told her to go get some rest to take her mind off of everything. She shared that she wanted to get into trauma-focused therapy, so I have compiled a list of female providers for her to check out. I think her starting therapy and being able to find comfort in Cash will be two things that will help her a lot as she navigates her thoughts and feelings.

A FEW HOURS LATER I FINISH MAKING DINNER and make my way upstairs to where Victoria is sleeping. She has opted to sleep in my bed since she wants to feel close to someone as she goes through her healing journey.

"Hey, Vic. Dinner is ready if you want to come downstairs and eat."

She slowly gets up and wipes her eyes, "can you give me a few minutes? I will be down in a few."

I do what she asks and head back to the kitchen, to get her plate ready for her.

When Joel wakes me up, I can feel a massive headache. It must be from all the crying that I have been doing today. I still can't believe I opened up completely to Joel about everything. I was relieved to see he didn't judge me and was willing to get resources together for me while I rested.

Despite the headache I have, I can smell something good coming from the kitchen.

I head into the bathroom, splash some water on my face, and take some headache medicine before going down the stairs.

"Something smells good," I say as I round the kitchen.

"I made some steak, green beans, and baked potatoes. I hope you enjoy it."

"Honestly, nobody ever cooks for me. I'm sure I will enjoy every part of this meal."

I sit down at the table and see a folder labeled "Vic"

on it. When I go to grab it, Joel says, "eat first then we can go over the folder and what all is in it."

"Okay, whatever you say."

We make small talk to catch up on life while we eat. "Damn, this is delicious. You definitely know how to cook," I blurt out.

Maybe I could have left the second part of it, but it is what it is at this point.

"Well thank you. I try sometimes." He says with a laugh.

ONCE WE FINISH EATING, I OFFER TO HELP HIM clean up the kitchen. It turns out he is the type of guy who cleans as he cooks, so all I had to do was the dishes we used for the meal. When we finish, we sit back down at the table with Joel directly next to me.

He opens the folder and says "so I have put a lot of different resources in here that I found while you were sleeping. I know how important starting therapy is to you, so I put in a few different providers that offer tele-health services. I also located OBGYNs that aren't far from the house, so you don't have to worry about us going out far. I will accompany you to any appointments that you have to ensure that you aren't alone. I've also added some coping skills that I have learned that seem to help patients when they enter the emergency depart-ment, so hopefully these will help some. I believe Detective Anderson wants us to come into the station tomorrow to get your formal statement of what happened. I'm sorry if this is a lot of information, but in the end having all of it will be worth it."

I don't know what comes over me, but I turn to face him and give him a big hug, while planting a kiss on his lips.

Fuck, why did I do that.

I jump up instantly, run upstairs to the bedroom, and lock myself in. I don't know why I did that.

CHAPTER 21

As Victoria and I were going through all of the information that I put together for her, she kissed me out of the blue. I feel so bad because she instantly ran away after it happened, which makes me feel that she is regretting what happened.

I head upstairs and knock on the bedroom door, where she locked herself in. "Vic, can I come in?"

"I'm so sorry, I truly didn't mean to do that. I am such a bad person," she starts to ramble.

"You are not a bad person at all. Sometimes when we get overwhelmed with emotions things happen randomly. Please let me in."

I can hear the door unlock and I slowly make my way in.

"Hey baby girl. I know emotions are running high right now. You are okay and I am not going to hold the kiss against you. Let's lay down and we can talk more about this tomorrow."

"Okay," she says, her voice low.

We climb into bed, and she snuggles up next to me. I rub her hair until she dozes off.

I don't want her to feel like she has to walk on eggshells in this house. I want it to feel like a home for her. A place where we can communicate openly when things are bothering us. I know it will take her time to be comfortable here, and with me.

If she tries to push me away, I'm still going to be by her side.

If she needs a shoulder to lean on, I will be that shoulder.

CHAPTER 22

The next morning comes, but this time I am awake before Joel is. I still feel a little embarrassed about my actions last night. It kind of just happened. I am thankful that he didn't make a big deal about it. Instead, he came and laid with me to help me calm down.

I look over at the clock and see it's seven in the morning. No wonder he's still asleep, it's too early for any normal person to be awake right now.

Instead of just lying in bed and wasting the day away, I decide to head downstairs and look into some of the therapy resources that Joel printed out. I make myself a cup of coffee while flipping through the different options. One therapist in particular stood out to me:

Kaitlyn Boyd, LCSW (she/her)

When conducting therapy I utilize a trauma-informed approach to meet the client where they are. I like to help clients navigate through their traumatic experiences and find coping skills that will help to reduce some of their symptoms to trauma.

Based on her bio, I think she is the one I want to book an appointment with. I set up my new laptop and went to the website to book an appointment with her. I have heard some people are able to get into therapy easily, while others have a long waitlist. Shockingly, Kaitlyn has an appointment at 2:00PM today. I go ahead and book the intake appointment with the hopes that she will be a good match for the concerns that I have.

Next, I decide to look at the different OBGYN doctors in the area to get on the books with them. With me being twelve weeks pregnant, I decided to book with Dr. Jewel Haynes, since she has the first available appointment on Friday. That's not bad at all since it's a couple days from now.

When I finish booking all the appointments that I need to, I look for the card Detective Anderson gave me. Wanting to be proactive, I decided to give her a call.

"Detective Anderson," she says when she picks up the phone.

"Hi Detective Anderson. This is Victoria who you met in the hospital."

"Yes. Hi Victoria. How are you feeling after a night's rest?"

"I am feeling a little better. Is it okay if I come around 10:00 to give my statement? I have an appointment at 2:00 that I don't want to miss."

"That's fine, I will see you then."

"See you then," I said, hanging up the phone.

I look back at the time and realize only an hour has gone by, so I decide to make my way to the stables to visit with Cash.

When I get to Cash, he's eating some straw, but it seems like he senses I'm here because he stops instantly and looks up.

Before I reach out to touch his head, I ensure that he sees me, so I don't startle him.

"Hey buddy. It's me again," I say before rubbing alongside his head.

"I hope it's okay if I spend a little bit of time with you and brush you again today. This morning has been busy with getting appointments scheduled, but I really feel like things are going to start to look up soon. You won't believe what happened yesterday. I was an idiot and kissed Joel out of nowhere. I know I shouldn't have done it, but there was just something in that moment that felt so right. Shockingly, he didn't overreact the way I did. I want to apologize to him, but I don't know where to start."

"Don't apologize," I hear a voice say.

I turn around to see Joel standing there looking sexier than ever.

"I thought you were asleep."

"I was, but the smell of fresh coffee in the house woke me up. I looked around the house, but I couldn't find you, so I figured you would be out here."

"Thanks for eavesdropping," I say with a laugh.

"I didn't want to interrupt you and your conversation with Cash, but I did want you to know that you don't have to be sorry." He says taking a couple steps closer, brushing aside a strand of hair from my face.

I can feel this unspoken tension in the air between the two of us. It's been less than forty-eight hours, and this man is just doing something to my body. It makes me want to cross that line again.

Before I can mess up and cross the line again, I turn back around and face Cash.

"Can I take him for a walk?" I ask as I continue to brush his coat.

"Yeah, let me get everything you need and you can take him around the path inside the gate.

CHAPTER 23

Joel

I know she can feel this tension between the two of us. The way she looks at me, makes me want to lean in and kiss her, but I know I shouldn't.

To break some of the tension I grab the reins for Cash and get them on him, so she has something to grab while she walks him.

"Alright, he's all ready for you," I announce.

"I feel dumb, but what do I do?"

"Don't feel dumb. This is your first time walking him." I show her what to do, and make sure she feels comfortable.

"That doesn't seem too bad. I think I'm ready. Oh, by the way, Detective Anderson would like to meet at 10:00 at the precinct to go through my statement."

"We can make that happen. It is a little after 8:00, so feel free to take him on a little walk then we can get ready to go."

The way she handles Cash makes her seem like a natural. This really shows how much they need one another, and how his presence is going to heal her. I truly am happy that she is getting the joy that she needs with him.

About twenty minutes pass by, I can see her bringing Cash back into the stables.

"How was it?" I ask.

"It was definitely needed. It helped provide me with some clarity of everything. I don't mean to keep hitting you with surprises today, but I was able to secure a 2:00 telehealth therapy appointment today and an OBGYN appointment on Friday at 9:00."

I'm glad I took the week off, so I can help her get to her appointment on Friday. I have a car that she can borrow, but I want her to feel comfortable driving in the area.

"I can help you get to your appointments on time. Let's head inside and get ready to go to the station."

She nods and takes the lead into the house.

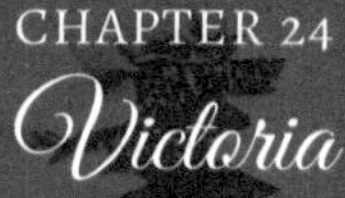

CHAPTER 24

Going for the walk with Cash was refreshing. I was able to experience the fresh, chilly air of November, but I was also able to take my mind off of what was going on around me.

It is a little daunting knowing that I was going to the police station to give my formal statement, but having Joel by my side helps to alleviate some of that stress.

After we both finish getting ready, we head to the car and make our way to the station.

With Joel living out in the middle of nowhere, it takes us about thirty minutes to get there. I look around and make sure there is no sign of Chase before hopping out of the vehicle. Joel can tell that I'm on high alert, so he makes his way to my door and grabs my hand.

"I got you baby girl. You will be safe. Let's head inside and get everything taken care of, then we can go to a diner down the road to eat."

"Okay," I say as I tighten my grip on his hand.

When I approach the front desk, I check-in and say, "I have an appointment with Detective Anderson."

The receptionist makes a call and within seconds, Detective Anderson is approaching us.

"Hi Victoria and Dr. White," she says, shaking our hands.

"You can just call me Joel, but nice seeing you again."

"Let's head this way and we can get started," she says, directing us towards the conference room.

AFTER TWO HOURS WE FINALLY FINISHED. It was difficult reliving all of the trauma I endured and explaining it to the detective. I do feel relieved that everything has been documented. Detective Anderson said she'll be taking out charges for assault and battery against Chase.

Although the protective order is still in place, I'm still nervous about what could happen if he gets his hands on me again. I know Joel is here to protect me, but he can't be with me all the time. Especially when he has to return to work.

"Vic, are you ready to get some food? I know today has been pretty heavy, but there is a really good diner down the street if you want to go. You have a little bit of time before your therapy appointment, and you need to get some food in your system," Joel says.

I'm nervous about going out in public since I know Chase has probably started to look for me, but I decide to go anyway. The baby and I both need food.

"Alright, let's go."

CHAPTER 25

Chase

After no luck finding Victoria yesterday, I decided to check into a local hotel so I could get some rest. With today being a new day, I get back on the hunt for her.

Who knows what she could have said or done so far. I hope she keeps her mouth shut. If not, she knows what consequences are coming for her.

Deciding that I need to eat something, I go to a diner that's right down the street from where I am staying. I remember them having good burgers from when we visited before.

I head inside and sit in a booth towards the back where I have a view of the whole restaurant. I ordered water with lemon and a mushroom swiss burger.

The only thing I hate about this diner is that the front door makes a ding every time someone comes in. Which seems like it's occurring way too often, until one ding changes everything.

There she is.

Victoria is in a pair of leggings with a blue hoodie on, entering the restaurant all alone. This is a seat yourself kind of place. I find it odd that she is just standing by the front door until an older man enters shortly after her. I've met her father before, and that's not him.

So, who the fuck is it.

The anger starts to build inside of me, until Victoria and I lock eyes with one another. I can see the panic start to form inside her, like she's seen a ghost. Every time she threatened to leave me; I reminded her that regardless of where she went I would find her.

Look at me now. In the same place, at the same time as her. Two hours away from our home.

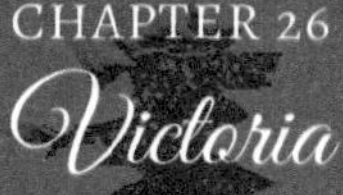

CHAPTER 26

Panic starts to rise inside me when I lock eyes with Chase. What the fuck is he doing here? I don't know how he found me or predicted that I would be here.

I don't know who I can trust anymore. Joel picked this place, so he must have known that Chase was going to be here. When Joel starts to move forward to one of the booths by the window, I dart for the exit and begin to run.

It's been a long time since I've been in this area, so I am sure that I will get a little mixed up with where everything is. Remembering that I have a new phone, I enter the address to the police station.

As I continue to run, I hear two voices yelling my name. Instead of looking back, I keep running until I get back to the station.

I am out of breath by the time I get there. When I get farther along in my pregnancy, I don't think I am going to be able to run like that anymore.

Once I catch my breath, I yell "He is here. He found me. I don't know what to do."

The receptionist looks so confused and calls two police officers in here who detain me.

"Why the hell am I being detained? I didn't do anything wrong. It's Chase Holden who did."

I must have been yelling super loudly because out of nowhere Detective Anderson is making her way into the lobby. "Why is she detained?" she asks, looking at the officers.

"She was acting out of control," one of the officers says.

"Uncuff her, NOW!" She yells loudly."Come on sweetie, let's go to my office and talk.

"Where's Joel?"

"Forget him. I think he set me up. When we got to the diner, Chase was there in a booth waiting for me. When we locked eyes, I just got up and ran. I don't want to be hurt again. I need to get out of here. I can't let him find out that I'm pregnant with his child. He can't get anywhere near me, or he's going to kill me this time."

"Slow down. What diner were you at? I can have some officers go out there." She says handing me some water.

"Gabby's Diner. I heard him calling after me, but I didn't look back. I just kept going."

She ends up putting in a request for officers to head to the diner to see if he's still there.

"We are going to figure this out together. Take some deep breaths and relax."

I do as she says, even though it's difficult at first. Right when I start calming down, she gets a call.

"Detective Anderson."

"Yeah, I understand."

"Thank you for letting me know."

I can only hear fragments of the conversation before she ends the call.

"Unfortunately, he was not there when officers arrived, but we did receive word that he was fighting with another man."

"Another man?" I ask.

"Yeah, it sounds like he was fighting with an older male who fits the description of Joel. Sweetie, I don't think he set you up. I think y'all were in the wrong place at the wrong time."

Shit, I should have known I overreacted.

"Why does this happen to me? I shouldn't have reacted the way that I did. I should have known that he was just trying to protect me and wouldn't do anything to harm me."

"Sometimes, after a traumatic event, individuals begin to develop negative thinking patterns. What you're experiencing is normal and it is a defense mechanism you are putting up to ensure you don't get hurt again. I do think you should hear him out," she says as she nods towards the door.

There he is. Showing up for me, even when I pushed him away.

CHAPTER 27

I should have known to not take Victoria out in public. Especially with it being days after the incident with Chase. I am stupid, and I deserve for her to hate me. I keep telling her that I was the one who was going to protect her, but clearly, I can't even do that.

When Victoria darted out of the diner, there was another man that tried to follow quickly after her. We made our way outside of the diner and I called his name "Chase," and he instantly turned around.

"Hasn't she made it clear that she wants nothing to do with you? She left you for a reason. You should just get the hint and go back home."

Clearly me saying that did not make him happy. He attempted to punch me in the face. Luckily, I have years of experience in boxing, so I blocked his punch and ended up hitting him in the face instead.

"You bitch. You're going to regret that," he says with blood dripping down his face.

"That was your warning to stay away. Next time, I

won't be as nice," I call after him as he runs toward his car.

I take note of the vehicle he's in and make my way to the police station, where Victoria's location is pinging at.

WHEN I ARRIVE AT THE STATION, I ASK TO GO TO Detective Anderson's office. I'm led directly there and see Victoria freaking out about the way she reacted. I know she's on edge lately and I should have taken that into consideration before we got into this situation in the first place.

When Detective Anderson points out I'm at the door, Victoria runs over to me, and I pull her into a hug.

"I'm so sorry. I didn't mean to," She starts saying. I cut her off by placing a finger on her lips.

"Shush, baby girl. We can talk about it when we get home. I just need to give Detective Anderson some information. Then we can get out of here, so you can get ready for your appointment."

An officer comes in and escorts Victoria to the snack area where she can eat something while I provide a statement to the detective.

"I'm sorry this has gotten out of control, but Chase was in the area. I might have punched him in the face, out of self-defense, when he started swinging at me. He did end up leaving in a blue four-door vehicle with license plate CDH99."

"From the look of your hand, I can tell something happened. We will pull the footage from the diner to corroborate your story. Just in case he decides to press charges. The information you gave will be very helpful. Now take Victoria home and make sure she takes it easy."

"Will do. Thank you for letting her come sit in your office."

"Of course. I will keep you both updated if I hear any additional information," she says walking me to the snack area to grab Victoria.

"Let's head home," I tell Victoria.

CHAPTER 28

When we get back to Joel's house, I look at the clock and realize it's already 1:30. I need to get ready for my therapy session soon.

While I get everything set up on the computer, Joel makes us some grilled cheese sandwiches since our lunch plans had been ruined by Chase. I'm very ready for this to be all over with, so I can move on with my life.

Instead of taking the time to talk about what happened, I grab my sandwich and laptop and head upstairs to my bedroom. Hopefully having this peace and quiet can help me out. Before my session begins, I have to fill out a PHQ and GAD-7 test to list symptoms that I experienced over the last two weeks. I know my scores are going to be severe on these tests, especially with the recent events that unfolded.

When 2:00 hits, I login to the telehealth appointment where Kaitlyn awaits.

"Good afternoon, my name is Kaitlyn Boyd, and I am a licensed clinical social worker who will be working with you today. Since this is our first session, we will be completing an intake assessment, and I'll be taking this time to get to know you more. Do you consent to tele-health treatment?"

"I do."

Throughout the session she asks a lot of questions to get to know me and why I ended up coming to therapy. I feel like the session was so smooth that I was able to open up and not feel judged by doing so. We ultimately decided to do weekly sessions for us to touch base and navigate what I went through and what I may continue to experience.

One component that we touched on today was my attraction that I am developing towards Joel. She high-lighted that sometimes after a sexual assault, individuals want to feel close to someone else and may become hypersexual or avoid sex and any type of relationships. She stressed the importance of having open communication with him and shared some coping skills that I can engage in if I start to feel overwhelmed with what is going on.

I really enjoyed the vibe my therapist gave off today, and I can't wait to see what next week will bring.

AFTER I CLOSE MY LAPTOP, I DECIDE THAT I need some water before I figure out what is next on my to do list. I hear a knock at the door, as if Joel was just waiting for me to finish.

"Hey Vic, can I come in?" Joel asks from outside the door.

"I guess," I shout back as I roam through my drawer to find a pair of pajamas.

"I am truly sorry for how things played out today, I put something together for you that I hope you will enjoy." He says while sticking out his hand for me to take.

After a few seconds of hesitation, I ended up grabbing his hand.

We make our way down the hallway, into the master bathroom. He has the bathroom set up with a shower steamer, soft music, sparkling grape juice, and some chocolate covered strawberries. I want to cry at the sight.

"I know you're still mad at me for what happened today, but I promise you, I didn't know that he was going to be there. I want you to take some time to take a hot shower to decompress after the day. I'll be back in a little to check on you."

"Thank you, Joel."

He heads out of the bathroom and shuts the door behind him.

I undress and slowly head into the shower, making sure I don't slip and fall over the step into the shower.

CHAPTER 29

I must've been in the shower for a while because I hear a knock at the door and Joel calling out "you good in there? It's been almost thirty minutes."

"I'm good, I will be out in a moment." I call back, grabbing one of the nearby towels to dry off.

After looking around for a few seconds, I spotted a robe with a note on top of it.

Vic,

I truly am sorry for what happened earlier today. I didn't mean to make you upset or hurt you in any way. I know this is one small thing that I did, but I hope to keep doing more. I want to show up for you when you're feeling stressed. I want to show up when you feel like you are hitting a breaking point. If you will allow me to, I want to be there during your happy moments too.

- Joel

I don't know what more he could do to put a smile on my face. The misunderstanding earlier was just that. *A misunderstanding.* I need to learn to take a breath and not jump to conclusions when things start to get hard.

I put the note aside and put the robe on, as I make my way into the bedroom. Joel is facing away from me, looking at his phone.

"Hey," I say, catching him by surprise.

"Hey, how was your shower?"

"It was needed, thank you so much for doing something special for me. I was never treated like this before. I'm very grateful that you're making me feel good about myself. Even if I might have upset you."

I can tell that it hit a nerve because he quickly makes his way over to my side of the room and places a finger under my chin, lifting up so I can make eye contact with him.

"You didn't upset me. You are healing and your reactions are on high right now. Please stop saying that and don't think for one second you need to apologize to me," he says.

I go to form words, but he kisses me before I can speak. I want to pull away at first, but don't. I feel like I should be triggered by this, but for some reason, I'm not.

I pull his shirt up over his head and I am awe struck by the sight of his chest.. This man is built so well. I run my fingers up and down his body, and I see the growing hunger in his eyes.

He goes to undo my robe but hesitates for a second.

"Is everything okay?" I ask.

"I don't want to rush anything. Whatever happens tonight, we can't turn back from."

"I know. I want you. I want to feel all of you. I want you to fuck me, so I can make new ones."

"Fuck. Vic. I'm telling you, once we start this, you're mine and I'm never letting you go."

"I don't want you to let me go. Please stop talking and fuck me already."

"Not so fast, pretty girl. I am going to take my time with you. I want you to know what it feels to be pleased by a real man."

With that, he pulls my robe off and admires my body.

"You're so damn beautiful," he says as he begins to plant kisses along my neck.

He slowly takes one of my nipples into his mouth and sucks gently on it. *Fuck this feels amazing.* He moves his fingers to my center and slowly rubs circles on my clit.

"Is this okay or should I stop?" He asks.

"Keep going," I say, letting out a moan.

For some reason, I'm enjoying his hands touching my body. He's creating a new mindset for me with the way that he touches me. Before I get lost in thought, he sticks one finger inside of me slowly moving in and out before sliding in a second finger.

The way his fingers feel inside me, makes me want so much more.

"Please fuck me."

"Not yet, pretty girl." He says as he slowly brings his face towards my dripping pussy.

He begins licking up and down my clit, as he continues to fuck me with his fingers.

I moan out his name as my fingers start to get tangled in his hair.

After he feels that I have been teased enough, he pulls his fingers out of me, reaches over to his nightstand, and pulls out a condom. He quickly pulls down his pants and sheaths himself.

God damn. The length and the girth of his cock catches me by surprise. He's bigger than Chase and I'm a little worried about the damage that he could do with that thing.

"Are you sure that monster cock is going to fit inside of me?" I say with a laugh.

"I will go slow. Lay back" he instructs.

With that, he moves on top of me and slowly inserts himself inside me.

"Fuck, I feel so full," I pant out.

He makes slow strokes in and out of me. "You take me so well, baby girl."

He starts to pick up his pace which makes me moan louder than I expected. The way he feels inside of me, is like nothing I have ever experienced before. The faster he goes, the more I can feel pressure building up inside of me.

Before I know it, I can feel my legs shaking and my pussy starts to pulsate around his cock. I wonder if this is what an orgasm is supposed to feel like because I've never had one before.

Shortly after I can feel Joel start to twitch inside me, a sign that he just reached his peak as well.

He sits like that for a couple of seconds before pulling out, pulling the condom off, and laying down next to me.

"Well damn, that was amazing. I've never had an orgasm before," I say.

He looks at me with shock filled eyes.

CHAPTER 30

I know this girl didn't just say she's never had an orgasm before. That douche bag clearly didn't know how to make a girl feel good. Now that she is with me, I am going to ensure that she has all the orgasms in the world. I've heard having sex while you're pregnant can be a good thing. I don't want to overdo it though and cause her more harm.

"That definitely won't be your last orgasm," I say, turning to face her.

I can see her facial expression change, as if she wants to cry.

"Did I do or say something wrong Baby Girl?"

She nods her head no. "It isn't you; it's me. I feel like I don't deserve you. You shouldn't have to sit and take care of me in the ways that you are. Something about us having sex just now really got my head spinning. I've never been treated the way that you treated me today. I don't know how to explain things. I'm just nervous that when my family finds out, they are going to resent you and get mad that you've been keeping this all a secret from them." She says before I interrupt her by planting a kiss on her lips.

"Look, don't be sad or afraid. We are going to figure this out day by day. I will be the person that you can wake up to everyday. I will be the person that you can lean on when times get hard. I will be the person that will ensure your body is taken care of. I will always be here, as long as you want me to."

I know this is all new for her, but I want her to feel as comfortable as she can. I don't want her to feel pressured doing anything she doesn't want to do either.

"So, what does this mean for us? I know I've only been here a few days, but you said that I was yours and you weren't letting me go. Was that just a spur of the moment saying, or did you actually mean it?" She says without looking at me.

I lift up her chin and turn her head slowly to face me. "Vic, I was being serious. I know this is all sudden, but I want to make things work with you and raise the baby with you. I don't want you to run again when things get tough."

"What about my father?"

"What about him?"

"He is your best friend. I know this isn't going to sit well with him."

"Who cares. I will show him how important you are to me and prove that I am willing to be with you every step of the way. Let me handle that when the time comes."

"Okay, if you say so. Can we head downstairs and get some food? I am starving after these festivities."

"I bet you are," I say laughing.

I get up from the bed and head down the hallway to retrieve her pajamas she picked out earlier and bring them back to her with a washcloth to clean her up.

"I'm going to wipe up some of this mess you have going on."

"Go for it," she says, opening her legs up for me.

Once we're all cleaned up, we head downstairs to grab some food before relaxing for the rest of the night.

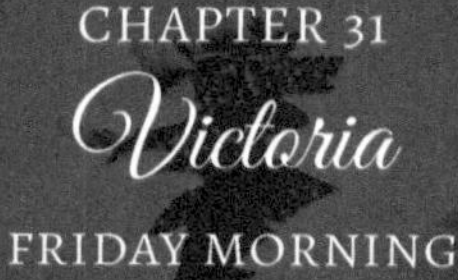

CHAPTER 31

FRIDAY MORNING

Since I get up earlier than Joel, I decide to head to the kitchen to get a morning snack.

I'm still in thinking of everything that happened the other night with Joel. The fact that we hooked up after me being here for a few days was so unexpected but so needed. I remember my therapist telling me that after a sexual assault I can become hypersexual, and I am already starting to see that in myself. Whenever we get a chance, we are banging like rabbits. I just love his body on mine.

Joel told me I could take a few days to think everything through and decide if I want to move forward with him or not. Part of me is a little nervous because I just got out of a ten-year relationship, but part of me feels like I am right where I'm supposed to be.

Today we have the first appointment with my OBGYN to get everything in place and ensure I have the right vitamins for having a successful pregnancy. One perk of living with a doctor is that he ensures I'm taking care of myself and I'm eating when I should be. It does suck that starting on Sunday he will be going back to work, and I can't spend as much time with him at home. He works overnight shifts currently, but he is trying to get on day shift, so I'm not alone at night.

"Good morning, Vic," Joel says, planting a kiss on my forehead when he gets into the kitchen.

"It's about time you get up and out of bed. We have less than an hour to get to my doctor's appointment."

"We'll make it on time. Let me grab a coffee for the road and we can head out."

"I'm a step ahead of you," I say while I hand him his travel mug with his usual black coffee.

<hr>

After our thirty-minute drive into the city, we arrived at the OBGYN office. I'm a little nervous because I don't know what to expect, but I'm sure everything will be okay.

When we get inside, I fill out the intake form with my medical history and general information. It only takes about five minutes before a provider calls me back."

I look over at Joel. He stands and takes my hand as we make our way back.

"Hi Ms. Maddox. My name is Julie, and I will be your nurse today. I am going to take your vitals and would like to get a urine sample to rule out any infections and confirm your pregnancy."

I nod in agreement, as she begins to take my blood

pressure, temperature, height, and weight. She ends up giving me a cup to pee in and shockingly I was able to.

After I'm done, I get escorted into a room where the ultrasound machine is located.

I think Joel can see the nerves on my face when she says "Baby girl, it's going to be okay. These are all routine things that they do during your appointments."

"I know. I am just nervous to actually see the baby and hear the heartbeat again. Last time it was still fresh in my mind, but now I have had a few days to process everything."

Before I get lost in my thoughts a knock sounds at the door.

"Good morning, my name is Rebecca and I will be your ultrasound tech today. We're going to take a look at your baby and see how everything is."

I nod in agreement.

"If you can lay back and lift your shirt up we will get started. This is going to be a little cold," she says as she begins to place the ultrasound gel on my stomach.

She moves the ultrasound wand around on my stomach, similar to what happened the other day in the hospital. Joel grabs my hand as we look at the screen and see the baby who appears to be a little bigger than what I saw last time.

"Let's see if we can hear a heartbeat," Rebecca says.

Boom. Boom. Boom.

Tears begin to well up in my eyes knowing that I can hear my baby's heartbeat. It feels so unreal because I didn't think that I would get to this point.

After we finish the ultrasound, I am moved to a different room where I wait for the doctor to come in.

* * *

"Good morning, my name is Dr. Haynes. You must be Victoria. May I ask who is accompanying you today?"

"This is Joel."

"Nice to meet you both. Is this your first baby?" She asks, looking between the two of us.

"Yes, it is but he isn't the biological father. I was actually in an abusive relationship and didn't know I was pregnant until a few days ago."

Shit. Maybe she didn't need all of that information, but it doesn't hurt to be honest.

"If you need any resources to help you support you through that process, then I can provide you with some."

"Thank you, but I think I'm good. I have been connected with resources and have started therapy, so I think that will help."

"Okay perfect, let's go ahead and review the intake form you filled out and take a look at your baby and see how everything is looking."

We finish going through the intake and review the ultrasound results.

"I was looking at your records in the health system and it says the doctor measured you at twelve weeks. It appears you are actually measuring at fourteen weeks. We will get you started on some prenatal vitamins and see you back in four weeks. Ensure that you keep your stress levels down as well to keep both you and the baby safe. Do you have any questions for me?"

I look over to Joel to see if he has any questions, but he nods no. "I don't think so. Thank you for getting me in so soon."

"Of course. If you need anything before the next visit, feel free to call the office. It was nice meeting you both again today."

ONCE WE FINISH UP THE VISIT, WE DECIDE TO swing through a drive thru to get something to eat. It might not be the healthiest option right now, but it is something.

As we get into the car, my phone starts to ring. I look down and see Detective Anderson's name appear on the screen.

"Hey Detective Anderson, is everything okay?" I ask answering the phone.

"Would you be able to stop by the station today? I want to talk to you about something."

I ask Joel how far we are from the station.

"We can be there in ten minutes."

"Okay, see you both then."

With that, I hang up and Joel places his hand on my leg. "It will be okay. Let's go see what updates she has to give, then we can get food and head home."

When we approach the police station, I feel super nervous. After the events that happened the other day, I can only imagine what she is going to tell us today. We make our way into the front lobby, Detective Anderson is waiting for us with a smile on her face.

"Hey Victoria and Joel," she says, extending her hand out for us to shake.

"Hey," I say, followed by Joel.

We head back to her office. The anticipation for what is to come, is really bothering me.

"Thank you both for coming in today. I want to start by saying you can take a deep breath; I have good news for you."

I look at Joel then back to the detective.

"Okay, go on please."

"Well after the incident at the diner the other day, we have had some patrol officers monitor the area just in case Chase reappears. This morning, we were told that he went back to the diner, so officers were able to pick him up on the assault & battery charge."

"That is good news, so what happens next?"

"He will be going to court in a few months and all of the evidence of what was done to you will be presented of what happened to you. I wanted to tell you this in person because you will have to testify. We will get you prepared beforehand, so you have an idea of what will be asked. I know this is a lot to take in right now, but do you have any questions for me right now?"

I'm at a loss for words, unsure of how I can face him head-on and explain everything that he did to me. I can barely cope with that alone right now, so how am I going to be able to keep it together enough to go through everything with him right in front of me.

"Right now, I don't really know how to feel. It is good that he is locked up right now, but I don't know how I feel about having to testify."

"I understand. It is a big ask, but having the jury and judge see your firsthand experience can help to ensure he doesn't do this again."

"Alright. Well, can I have some time to think about everything? I don't know how to feel. I'm glad he's locked up, but I'm concerned about having to testify"

"Absolutely. I just wanted to keep you in the loop of what things are going to look like moving forward. Remember if you have any questions, you can always contact me. I will be in touch."

"Thank you," I say, standing to walk out of the building.

WHEN WE GET BACK INTO THE TRUCK TO HEAD and get some food, I'm still at a loss of words.

"How are you feeling, baby girl? I know that was a lot of news to take in."

"Honestly, I don't know how to feel. I feel connected to him, especially being pregnant with his child. Part of me doesn't want him to be behind bars, but the rest of me knows it's necessary. It's all just so confusing and complicated."

"That is a completely normal reaction. You have every right to feel that way. We can navigate this process together and go from there."

"Thank you, Joel. You really mean a lot to me. Maybe it's just my attachment style, but there is just something about you that I don't want to lose."

He squeezes my leg and kisses my forehead. "Let's go get some food and head home."

Home. I love that word. It makes me feel like I am actually wanted in a space.

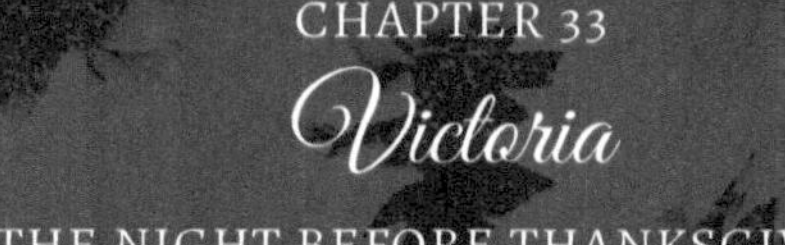

CHAPTER 33

Victoria

THE NIGHT BEFORE THANKSGIVING

The past few weeks have been great. Joel and I have gotten closer, and we decided to officially start dating. I know to some people this might seem fast because I just got out of a long relationship, but the more I reflect on it, I don't even feel like that relationship was real. I feel like I was just there to be used for Chase's enjoyment.

With Joel, he makes me feel special and truly wanted. When he went back to work it was a little rough being in bed alone with my thoughts, but with some convincing he was able to get moved to day shift. This allows us to finally be able to go to bed together and make me feel comfortable.

I have been seeing a therapist and a psychiatrist. My psychiatrist started me on Lexapro and Buspar for my anxiety and depression, which has started to help me feel leveled out. It was important to ensure that I can be on the medications while pregnant, but they said those were fine, so I went with it.

During my last therapy appointment, I navigated how to tell my parents about my pregnancy and my relationship with Joel. My therapist and I did some role-playing exercises which seemed to help a little, but I am still nervous about what they will think. We talked about doing some deep breathing if I start to feel overwhelmed when I navigate the conversation.

Today I know I need to work up the courage to call my parents and let them know that I am back in town and see if they are open to me coming over for dinner tomorrow for Thanksgiving. I have been dreading this moment, but Joel told me he would be by my side to navigate Thanksgiving dinner if I get the invite.

I know this is an untraditional relationship, especially because he is my father's best friend, but I can't help that I am falling for him. People always say you find your person in the most untraditional ways, and I think that is what happened here between the two of us.

"Hey baby girl, watcha thinking about?" Joel says as he plants a kiss on my forehead.

"Just how to break this news to my parents about everything going on. I want them to be proud of me and everything, but I am afraid they are going to have a negative reaction. What if things get wild and you get targeted for being with me?"

"We will cross that bridge if we get to it. I think your parents will understand and be there for you. Vic, you're a mom. That's a huge step. They are going to be grandparents. Even though this wasn't a planned pregnancy, I'm sure they will support you. How about this... you call your parents today, tell them you're back in town, and see what they have planned for tomorrow. I'll sit here with you while you have the conversation if you need me."

"Okay. I can do that. My mom's phone number was one that I memorized if I ever needed it." I say, dialing her number.

After a few rings, she picks up "hello."

"Mom, it's Victoria."

"Victoria, is everything okay? I've been trying to get in contact with you, but your phone would just go straight to voicemail."

"It's a long story, but I am doing okay now. What are y'all doing for Thanksgiving tomorrow?"

"We're staying at home. We can make dinner if you would like to come over. You can bring Chase with you."

"He won't be coming with me, but I will be there. Can you send me the time and location?"

"Of course I can. I really hope things are going well for you. I will see you tomorrow."

"I will explain everything tomorrow. I love you. Tell dad I love him too."

"We love you too sweetie."

I take a deep breath because I know the conversation tomorrow is going to be a heavy one.

"Vic, I'm here and remember I will be with you while you have that conversation tomorrow too," he says as he takes my hand into his.

"Thank you. You've saved me and you continue to save me every day."

My phone dings and I see a message from my mom.

Mom: Let's do 4pm tomorrow. Our address is: 1302 Pacific Rd

Me: See you tomorrow 

I google the address and see they only live fifteen minutes away from Joel. I don't know how everyone likes the country living. I know it's a huge adjustment for me since I've always been a city person.

CHAPTER 34

Victoria

Trigger Warning: Mention of Miscarriage (Not FMC)

I woke up this morning and just laid in bed. Joel decided to pick up a shift from 3AM-11AM to help out since nobody wanted to work the early morning shift. Luckily, I was able to continue to sleep with him gone, but I am anticipating his arrival soon.

Today is going to be a nerve-wrecking day, even though my therapist prepared me for what to expect on both the good side and the bad side. My mom seemed like she was excited for me to come home for Thanksgiving, but that might change when she sees who I am bringing with me.

It's like he knew I was thinking about him. I hear Joel walking in through the front door. He heads upstairs and notices me just lying in the bed.

"I would come hop in with you, but I need to take a shower first."

"Yeah, wash your funky ass. I'll be here when you're done," I say with a laugh.

About ten minutes later, Joel comes out of the shower and jumps in bed butt ass naked.

"What do you think you're doing?"

"Doing you if you would like me to," he laughs and comes over and starts planting kisses along my body.

"Shouldn't you be getting ready to take a nap?"

"I should, but you're more appealing to me than a nap right now. So, what do you think?"

"I think you should stop talking and come fuck me."

"Say less," he says, grabbing a condom from the nightstand.

He goes down on me before fucking the shit out of me. Feeling his touch never gets old. I can't wait to continue to experience this with him for years to come.

Once we finished, he cuddles up beside me and drifts off to sleep. I grab my e-reader and read for a few hours before waking Joel up to get ready for tonight.

Shockingly, you still can't tell that I'm pregnant. I threw on a long sleeve tan sweater dress with black leggings. I decided to throw a black scarf with it because the weather has gotten a little cold recently. Joel on the other hand is being boring and wore a black sweater with black jeans.

The jitters inside of me for how the rest of the night is going to go are really getting to me, and I can tell Joel notices.

"Let's take a deep breath in and out. Tonight is going to go well. It's been a while since your parents have seen you, so I'm sure they will be happy to see you again. You look beautiful. I think you can get away with them not knowing you are pregnant right away too, but I will say you are glowing. We will see how things go."

"Thank you, babe," I say while planting a kiss on his lips.

We sit on the couch and watch an episode of reality TV before it becomes time to head out.

"You ready?" Joel asks.

"As ready as I can be."

We head to his truck and make our fifteen-minute drive to my parents' house.

Once we pull up to their house, I take a few more deep breaths before I head to their door.

"Alright, it's time," I say while ringing the doorbell.

My father opens the door and before saying hello to me, he looks at Joel and asks, "what are you doing here?"

Before Joel can respond, I interject and say, "well hello to you to dad. Can we come in and I can explain everything?"

"I want to know why he is here first with you."

"Hey Victoria," Mom says as she pushes past dad. "Joel, why are you here?"

"How about y'all stop asking and you just let us inside, so I can fill you in on everything."

Dad looks angry, but mom moves him out of the way and says "Come in. Dinner is ready, so we can talk at the table.

After we each get our plates of food, we make our way to the kitchen table. Mom and Dad sit across from Joel and I.

"So, who is going to explain why my daughter is here with my best friend," Dad says before I can get anything else out.

"Hun, give her a second. She just got here, you can at least make her feel welcome."

Dad rolls his eyes and starts eating his food.

"Since that's the only thing dad cares about rather than asking how his own daughter is doing, I will just go ahead and say it. Joel and I have been in a secret relationship for the past few weeks. I ran away from Chase and I'm pregnant."

Maybe I didn't have to be so blunt about everything, but I needed to get it off my chest since dad would have kept bothering me if I didn't get to the point.

Dad stands from his seat and quickly comes to our side and punches Joel. "What the fuck do you think you are doing getting my daughter pregnant? You know she is the one person who is completely off-limits to you. How could you just go and betray me? I want you out of my fucking house."

Instead of Joel reacting in the same manner as my father, he just stands up and wipes the blood coming out of his nose.

"ENOUGH," I yell out.

This causes everyone to look at me.

"Joel did not get me pregnant, Chase did. I've been a victim of his abuse for ten years now. A few weeks ago, I finally worked up the courage to escape him, hence why I am back in town. When I went to the emergency room, Joel was there working a shift. He offered to take me in to get me back on my feet when I found out I was pregnant. Ever since then we just got closer and decided to make things official between us. I made him promise me that he wouldn't tell y'all that I was back because I didn't want to seem like a failure, but clearly that wasn't the right decision." Tears start to stream down my face.

My father tries to come over to comfort me, but I pull away. "Don't you dare put your hands on me after the way you reacted."

"I'm sorry Vic. I overreacted and didn't know the full story."

"You're just saying sorry to make yourself feel better about your actions. If this is how the night is going to go, then we're leaving."

"No sweetie, stay. We haven't seen you in a long time and I want to catch up with you. I'm so sorry I wasn't there for you while you were navigating everything with Chase, but I am here now. Just let me know what you need. Also, congratulations on the baby. You are going to be an amazing mother," Mom says to me.

"I wanted to tell you, but I didn't want you to think less of me. I know y'all are mad about the situation with Joel, but I really love him. He has been here for me through everything and has kept me safe from Chase. Luckily, Chase has been arrested, so that is one less thing I have to worry about, but I will have to face him in a few months at court. Dad, I know Joel is your best friend, but he really cares about me. He hasn't done anything to harm me. I know it's going to take you some time to understand why I chose him, but trust me... I did it with good reason."

Fuck, I just said I love Joel. I haven't even told him that myself.

I can see my father's demeanor change some.

"Victoria, I truly am sorry I overreacted. I want what's best for you. Joel I'm sorry for punching you. Can we give the girls a few minutes to talk, and we talk in the kitchen?"

Shockingly, Joel agrees. He kisses me on the forehead and heads into the kitchen with my father.

Mom and I are sitting at the kitchen table, and she begins with "are you sure that you are okay? I never told you but the person that I was with before your father was abusive to me. I ended up getting pregnant, but one night he attacked me so badly that I had a miscarriage. I'm telling you this to say that I know what you have been through, and I will be there for you every step of the way. I will admit it is going to be an adjustment at first with Joel and you being together, but if you're happy, then I am happy. I'm sure your father will come around too."

"Thank you, mom. I am thankful for you and your support. Everything is still new with the baby and the relationship with Joel, but I am excited to see where everything goes from here. I feel so much happier with him than I was with Chase. Speaking of him, he was arrested on charges of assault and battery. I will have to go to court in the upcoming months to testify, so if you can be there for that, then I would really appreciate it."

"Of course. Whatever you need, just let me know."

We continue talking about everything that happened with Chase and how I have started therapy. Mom commended me on getting help because it was one thing that she didn't do, that she wished she had.

"Once you get acclimated again, I hope you can find a good work from home job. I switched over to a job where I don't have to leave my house, and it's been a lifesaver. I only have to dress from top up since nobody sees the bottom half. That's the freedom of working from home."

"Yeah, Joel and I haven't talked too much about job options, but I am thinking about going back to school to get my Bachelor's in Social Work. I want to be able to help other survivors of domestic and sexual assault, so I hope having that degree will allow me that opportunity."

"I can see you being a great social worker one day. You have always been determined and passionate, so being in that career you can use those skills. Even though this isn't a situation that anyone should be in, you will be able to connect with those survivors on a different level than others."

"You're right about that. I will have to look into all the different paths and see what makes the most sense, then I could always get a part-time job from home while completing the degree."

"I think that's a good path to take. Let's call the guys back in. I hope your dad didn't try to kill Joel in there."

"I hope not. I can't lose the one man who is bringing me some sanity again," I say laughing.

CHAPTER 35

I can't believe Brian really decided to punch me in the face when he found out about Victoria and I. Casey even let it happen, which is even more shocking to me.

When Brian pulled me aside in the kitchen, I was scared for what was to come. I thought he would make me never see Victoria again, but instead the conversation went a completely different way.

"Joel, I'm sorry for the way I acted. I shouldn't have punched you. Instead, I should have listened and got both sides of the story. I know I overreacted. I hope that won't change the relationship between us or the relationship with my daughter. I will be completely honest with you, it is going to take a little bit of time for me to adjust to this whole thing of my best friend dating my daughter, but I'm sure over time I will get used to it."

"You're good. I'm sure I would have reacted the same way. I do want you to know I truly care about Vic. She has been through a lot, and she finally feels safe with me. I will never take advantage of her. Instead, I will ensure that she has everything that she needs and not treat her the way that douche bag did."

"Speaking of him. What happened there?"

"All I know is when Vic came into the hospital that Sunday night she was bent out of shape. She had bruises all along her body. She did get a thorough exam, and charges pressed with one of the detectives. Chase hurt her badly, both physically and mentally, but she is starting to get better with the help of a therapist and psychiatrist."

"Chase is going to be dead if I get my hands on him."

"That's the same way that I felt, but he is luckily in jail so he shouldn't be going anywhere near her again."

"Good. One question for you. Do you love Victoria?"

I pause for a second because we have never spoken those words out loud to one another before.

"Brian, I really do. We haven't said it yet, but I know she feels my love. Honestly, I have been looking for the right time to say it to her."

"I recommend you do it sooner than later, so you know how she feels. You know us Maddox's are not the best with words sometimes. You might have to be the one who starts that conversation."

"Yeah, I might need to. Thank you again for understanding why we are together. She is really going to need you these next few months and years to come. I hope you're ready to be a grandpa," I laugh while nudging him in the shoulder.

Before he can respond, Casey calls out "the food is getting cold, y'all better come and eat."

We give each other a hug and make our way back to the kitchen table.

"I hope y'all had a good chat." Victoria says while looking between Brian and me.

"Something like that. Your dad has a good right hook," I say with a laugh.

"I hope he never has to use it again," she says.

Everything seems to go back to normal. We are all making conversations with one another and there is so much laughter throughout the room. I truly am thankful that we have been able to all spend this time together.

I get pulled from my thoughts when Brian asks a question.

"Joel how has everything being going in the stables? I'm sure Victoria would have a good time engaging with the different horses."

"She has actually bonded nicely with one of my newer horses Cash. He was a recent rescue that went through a similar situation as her."

"Yeah, the first day that I met him we instantly connected. I never thought I would be a horse person, but for some reason I am."

"That's good sweetie. Maybe next time y'all can have us over for dinner, so I can meet Cash," Casey says.

"I'm fine with whatever Victoria wants to do. I think it would be great if we could have y'all over for dinner.

"Alright, enough about the horses. How about we have some of mom's famous apple pie. I was able to smell it as soon as we walked through the front door" Victoria says.

Casey nods her head in agreement and goes to the

kitchen to go grab the pie. When she returns she brings left, right, center for us to play as well. This is going to be great because my luck always seems to be going in the right direction when I play this game.

I look over to Victoria as she eats her pie and I see the biggest smile on her face. I am so happy to see the joy in her eyes that I wasn't able to see when we first reconnected.

AFTER A FEW HOURS OF CATCHING UP, EATING desserts, and playing some games, we decide it is time to head home for the rest of the night. I can tell Vic is tired, so I don't want to keep her up all night when we get home.

"Thank you both for having us over tonight," I say.

"Of course. It was good seeing y'all again. Don't be strangers" Casey says.

"I'm sorry again for what happened early in the night. I really didn't mean for things to get out of hand. I hope your nose is okay and it's not broken," Brian says.

"I hope not either. I can't look at an ugly man every-day," Vic says with a laugh.

"Hey, you like me whether I'm ugly or not," I joke with her.

"Yeah yeah. Well mom and dad, I love y'all. I will defi-nitely keep in touch," she says.

We all give each other hugs, and we head out for the night.

We take the fifteen-minute drive back home, and she instantly heads upstairs and changes into her pajamas. When I climb into bed, she decides to make small talk before we head to sleep.

"Well, I guess tonight ended up going well in the end. I'm sorry about your face though, I didn't think my dad was going to react that way. I am glad my parents are here to support me with the baby and the court case. I'm thankful for you all."

"I'm thankful for you too. We both prepared for the good and the bad to happen tonight. I'm pretty sure I'm good with no breaks, but it might be swollen for a little bit. Now don't worry about me. Get some rest, and we can talk more in the morning."

"Okay, you try to get some rest too since you have to work tomorrow. I love you," she says as she turns over.

"I love you too."

Shit. I just told her I love her. I hope she knows I mean it and I'm not just saying it to say it after the day we had.

I used that word again. I told him I loved him, and he actually said it back to me. My heart is beating so fast that I want to just hop over to him and kiss him non-stop, but I don't want him to see the way it is making me feel. Instead, I am going to head to sleep, and we can address it another day.

Did you enjoy this story? Are you looking for more of Victoria and Joel? Are you looking to see what happens to Chase?

Well, definitely stick around.

The next book will be coming soon.

Acknowledgments

Thank you all for picking up my book and reading it! This book touches on darker subjects, but thank you for sticking around and getting through it.

I would like to thank Alicia Ramos for sprinting with me constantly to help me get this book out to the world.

Thank you to my alpha readers Ava, Hilary, Emma, Rachel for helping me perfect this book for readers.

Thank you to my street team for helping me push my books out, so people can know who I am and what I write!

Thank you to Britt Lynn for creating this beautiful cover that incorporates my love for sunflowers in it.

Deann Soleil

About the Author

Deann Soleil is a self-published author based in Virginia who focuses on writing forbidden romances. When not writing, she is a full-time social worker who works with victims of community violence to help them overcome their traumatic experiences. If you're looking for short, fast-paced books, then look no further.